# READING POWER

## Transportation Through the Ages

# Cars of the Past

### Mark Beyer

The Rosen Publishing Group's
PowerKids Press™
New York

Published in 2002 by The Rosen Publishing Group, Inc.
29 East 21st Street, New York, NY 10010

First Edition

Book Design: Christopher Logan

Photo Credits: Cover © Robert Holmes/Corbis; p. 4 © AP/Wide World Photos/Ford Motor Company; p. 5 © AP/Photo; pp. 6, 7 © AP/Wide World Photos/The National Automotive History Collection; pp. 8, 9 © AP/Wide World Photos/Ford Motor Company; p. 11 © AP/Wide World Photos/Ford Motor Company; p. 12 © Bettmann/Corbis; p. 13 © AP/Wide World Photos/Library of Congress; pp. 14, 15 © Superstock; p. 16 © Bettmann/Corbis; p. 16 © Hulton Deutsch Collection/Corbis;p. 16 © Kim Sayer/Corbis; p.17 © Image Bank; pp. 18, 19 © Superstock; pp. 20, 21 © AP/Wide World Photos/Reed Saxon

Beyer, Mark.
Cars of the past / by Mark Beyer.
   p. cm. – (Transportation through the ages)
Includes bibliographical references and index.
ISBN 0-8239-5983-X (library binding)
1. Automobiles–History–Juvenile literature. [1.
Automobiles–History.] I. Beyer, Mark. Transportation through the ages.
II. Title.
TL206 .C48 2001
629.222'09-dc21
                                                    2001000153

Manufactured in the United States of America

# Contents

## The First Cars

Henry Ford made this car in 1896. It had a small engine. Drivers used a handle to turn this car.

Handle

Engine

**Henry Ford**

Cars soon became more useful. This car had a top, windows, and lights. Now people could drive in the rain. They could also drive at night.

**Windows**

**Lights**

Top

This car was made in 1905.

# Building Cars

Many people helped build
each car. Each person had one job.
Cars were made fast this way.

This was a car factory in 1912.
A car was made in 93 minutes.

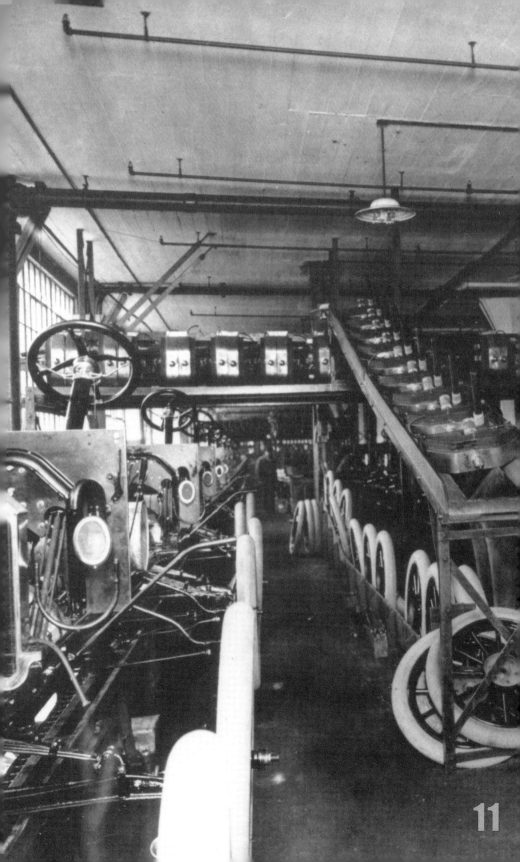

# Different Kinds of Cars

This is a Model T. It sold for $290.

1923
Model T

Some cars were big.
This car could seat six people.

**1923
Sedan**

This car had a roof that went up and down. This car was called a sports car.

I like to ride with the top down.

**1936 British Sports Car**

Some cars were long. Some cars were fancy. Some cars were small.

1963
Convertible

1960
Sports Car

1965
Compact Car

# On the Road

By the 1930s, cars had radios and clocks.

Radio

Clock

By the 1950s, cars had seat belts.
Seat belts helped to keep
people safe.

Seat belt

By the 1960s, most families had a car. Highways were built around the country. There were many different cars on the road.

People love old cars. Cars of the past are more popular than ever.

1947
Luxury Car

# Glossary

**British** (**briht**-ihsh) of or about Great Britain or its people

**compact** (**kahm**-pakt) a car smaller than most models

**convertible** (kuhn-**ver**-tuh-buhl) a car with a folding top

**engine** (**ehn**-juhn) the motor that powers a car

**factory** (**fak**-tuhr-ee) a place where things are made

**handle** (**han**-dl) the part of something that you hold on to with your hand

**highways** (**hy**-wayz) main public roads

**luxury** (**luhk**-shuhr-ee) something that is pleasant but not necessary

**seat belts** (**seet behlts**) belts that hold someone in a seat

# Resources

**Books**

*Eureka! It's an Automobile!*
by Jeanne Bendick
Millbrook Press (1994)

*Eyewitness: Car*
by Richard Sutton
Dorling Kindersley Publishing (2000)

**Web Site**

Cars and History at the Sloan Museum
http://www.ipl.org/exhibit/sloan/

# Index

**C**
clocks, 17

**E**
engine, 4

**F**
factory, 10
Ford, Henry, 4–5

**H**
handle, 4
highways, 19

**R**
radios, 17

**S**
seat belts, 18

**Word Count:** 182

**Note to Librarians, Teachers, and Parents**

If reading is a challenge, Reading Power is a solution! Reading Power is perfect for readers who want high-interest subject matter at an accessible reading level. These fact-filled, photo-illustrated books are designed for readers who want straightforward vocabulary, engaging topics, and a manageable reading experience. With clear picture/text correspondence, leveled Reading Power books put the reader in charge. Now readers have the power to get the information they want and the skills they need in a user-friendly format.